D1190581

WITHDRAWN FROM
COLLECTION

Where Is the Night Train Going?

Bedtime Poems

by Eileen Spinelli

Illustrated by Cyd Moore

MANDAN PUBLIC LIBRARY
108 1st Street NW
MANDAN, NORTH DAKOTA 58554

Wordsong
Boyds Mills Press

To my grandchildren, sweet poems rewriting themselves each day

— E.S.

For Milton and Mildred, the grandparents of my children, with great respect and love

—C.M.

Text copyright © 1996 by Eileen Spinelli
Illustrations copyright © 1996 by Cyd Moore

All rights reserved

Published by Wordsong
Boyds Mills Press, Inc.
A Highlights Company
815 Church Street
Honesdale, Pennsylvania 18431
Printed in Mexico

Publisher Cataloging-in-Publication Data
Spinelli, Eileen.
   Where is the night train going? / bedtime poems by Eileen Spinelli ; illustrated by Cyd Moore.—1st ed.
[32]p. : col. ill. ; cm.
Summary : A collection of poems that appeal to the imagination of young
children. Bright watercolor drawings accompany each poem.
ISBN 1-56397-171-2
1. Imagination—Children's poetry. 2. Children's poetry, American.
[1. Imagination—Poetry. 2. Poetry, American.] I. Moore, Cyd, ill. II. Title.
811.54—dc20   1996   AC
Library of Congress Catalog Card Number 94-79162

First edition, 1996
Book designed by Tim Gillner
The text of this book is set in 17-point New Caledonia.
The illustrations are done in colored pencil and watercolors.
Distributed by St. Martin's Press

10 9 8 7 6 5 4 3 2 1

CONTENTS

WHERE IS THE NIGHT TRAIN GOING?

Where is the night train going?
Oh, may I go along?
I'd like to see the mountains
And sing a mountain song.
I'd like to ride past rivers
Past sleepy-shadowed farms.
I'd like to see the whole wide world
Within the night train's arms.

SILVER

Silver is best
At night
When the lights
On boats and bridges
Look like bracelets,
When the fish flash silver
In the lonely lake,
And the moon
Is a shimmering puddle
In the sky.

Silver is best
After dark
When the breeze
In the park
Is silver-cool,
And the first star—
Light-years away—
Silvers in the night,
Taking wishes.

7

ART

Down in the dumpster
The artist sees—
In spools of wire
And hooks and keys
In pipes and springs
And iron pans
In curtain rods
And rusted cans—
A sculpture suited
For a park.
Down in the dumpster
Deep and dark.

8

SAFE

I keep all my treasures very safe
As safe as safe can be
(My silver dime, my autographs,
My secret-diary key,
My Florida shells, my Utah salt,
And my Montana rocks).
Who'd ever dare to look for them
Among my dirty socks!

MANDAN PUBLIC LIBRARY

I'D RATHER SLEEP AT THE ZOO

What could be worse
Than a lion who roars?
What could be worse—
A brother who snores!

THE GREAT WHITE SHARK

The great white shark is fierce and fast
With teeth as hard as steel.
He's known to chew a boot or boat
Or raincoat for a meal.
The great white shark scares lots of folks
Especially in the dark,
But I can tell you *nothing*
Ever scares the great white shark.

COUNTING SHEEP TO GET TO SLEEP

The first sheep jumps the fence and then
Turns around and jumps again.
The second sheep won't jump at all.
The third hides in the horse's stall.
The fourth sheep eats the scarecrow's hat.
The fifth goes dancing with the cat.
The sixth one drives the farmer's truck.
The seventh sheep quacks like a duck.
The eighth is late, the ninth pours tea,
The tenth climbs into bed with me.
The next time I can't get to sleep
I'll try warm milk—not counting sheep.

MOON

When the moon is full
And its face is round
Then it finds me where
I can be found
In my small, dark bed
In the dead of night
And it dishes me down
A plate of light
And I lap it up
Like a cat laps cream
Till I fall asleep
In a moon-bright dream.

STORM WARNING

When the storm comes
We will run
To the house
Slam the door
Peek through the curtains
Jump at the thunder
Screech at the lightning
Hide under the covers
Shiver and giggle
Together like cousins.
Mother will bring
Steaming hot chocolate
And slices of cake—
We'll have a party
To the tune of the rain
When the storm comes.

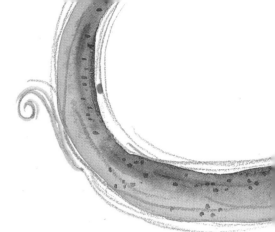

QUESTIONS FOR A NIGHT WATCHMAN

What do you see on your night watch?
What do you hear on your rounds?
Cats and bats and night owls?
Creaky-footstep sounds?
Do you always feel brave in the darkness?
Do you bump into walls by mistake?
Have you ever chased after a shadow?
And how do you stay awake?

I DON'T BELIEVE IN BIGFOOT

I don't believe in Bigfoot
Or skeletons that dance.
I don't believe in werewolves
Or zombies in a trance.
I don't believe in Martians
Or ghosts in sheets of white.
I don't believe in witches,
Who ride their brooms at night.
I don't believe in vampires
Or monsters from the sea—
And I'm hoping with my fingers crossed
They don't believe in me.

BEING ALONE

Alone can be drawing a flower in bloom
Or rearranging the toys in your room
Or taking a walk in the whispery snow
Or planting an acorn and watching it grow.
Alone can be curling up with a book
Or looking for tadpoles and frogs in a brook
Or merrily dancing where no one can see.
Alone can be building a house in a tree
Or it can be sailing up high on a swing
Or flying a kite on the end of a string.
Alone can be splashing in puddles of rain
Or waving to passengers riding the train
Or counting on fingers each bright evening star
Or trying to learn about just who you are
Or dreaming of things that are yet to be done.
Alone can surprise you—
Alone can be fun!

IN DEEP

Here's a field of goldenrod
Tiptoe in
Feel the tickle
On your knees,
Your belly,
And your chin.
Sneeze once
Sneeze twice
Scamper out
Behind the mice.

STORING STUFF

Bees store honey made from roses.
Clowns store whistles, wigs, and noses.
Mice store tidbits from the cat.
Aunt Jane stores last season's hat.
Farmers store their corn and hay.
Brides store bridal gowns away.
Dogs store bones, and sharks store teeth—
A row on top, a row beneath.
Squirrels store nuts from autumn trees.
I store happy memories.

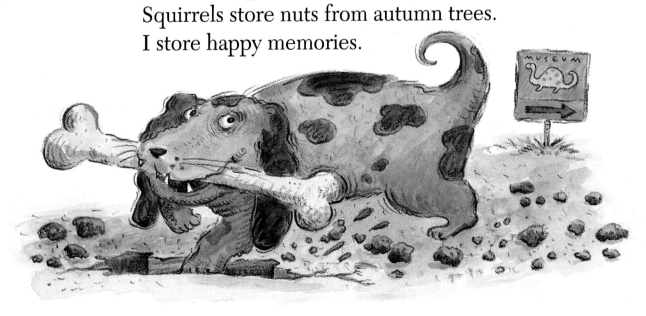

MOVING

We are moving away
So I must say good-bye
To my room and my swing
And that sweet part of sky
That sometimes hangs blue
And sometimes hangs gray
Over the fields
Where I used to play.
Good-bye to my old friends
Jason and Sue
They wave from their porches,
Are they crying too?
The moving truck rumbles
Past all that I know—
The school and the woods
And the creek down below.
And everything seems
To be pleading
"Don't go!"

SHOWTIME

Come the starry stage of night
Fireflies
Asleep all day
Splash into a song of night
Dance a sparkling ballet.

EARTHSONG

Aboard
The spacecraft
Voyager
On a golden disc
The humpback whale
Sings haunting sea songs.
Songs sail along
Through years
Of dancing light
To stars
Planets
Galaxies.

Who is listening?

AUGUST BEDTIME

Scent of apple
Scent of pear
Scent of darkness
In the air.

Breathing starlight
Dreaming moon
Lullaby's
A cricket tune.

Back-porch hammock
Soft and deep
Sways me into
Summersleep.

WINGS

I have no wings
With which to fly
But I can sail
The sweeping sky
And I can soar
Above the sea
On borrowed wings
Of poetry.

LAST SUMMER

Last summer
When everyone else
Had gone home and
The beach was
Quiet,
We drove near the ocean—
Bump-bump-bump—
In my father's old blue truck,
And we waved to the gulls
And we sang to the moon
And my mother fed us
Jelly sandwiches from
A basket on the front seat
And my baby brother
Fell asleep all sweet and sticky.
It's what I dream about—
That summer-bump ride on the sand—
Now that it's cold
And winter.

RAINY GRAY DAYS

Rainy gray days
Are for cuddling down
Snug in a sweater
Or a long dressing gown,
Sleepy-eyed, yawning,
Slippered and slow,
Puttering, buttering
Crackers to go
With strawberry jam
And a nice pot of tea,
Looking out windows
Imagining sea,
Humming a shanty
Of sailor and storm,
Tapping to music
The raindrops perform.

SURPRISE

I can feel the chill,
I can sense the dazzling light
Of the unexpected snow
That came down last night.
Oh, the unexpected joy
Of awaking to a day
That is hushed and new,
Just a windowpane away.